For Sara
H. P.

For Olivia
E. S.

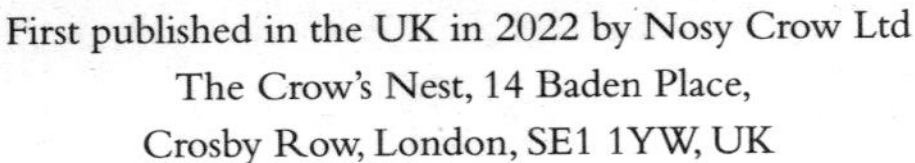
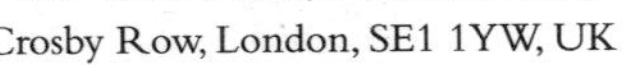

First published in the UK in 2022 by Nosy Crow Ltd
The Crow's Nest, 14 Baden Place,
Crosby Row, London, SE1 1YW, UK

Nosy Crow Eireann Ltd
44 Orchard Grove, Kenmare,
Co Kerry, V93 FY22, Ireland

ISBN: 978 1 83994 279 2

A CIP catalogue record for this book will be available from the British Library.

Printed and bound in Great Britain by Clays Ltd, Elcograf S.p.A.

Papers used by Nosy Crow are made from wood grown in sustainable forests.

1 3 5 7 9 10 8 6 4 2

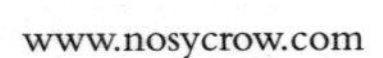

www.nosycrow.com

A Seal Pup Called Pearl

HELEN PETERS

illustrated by

ELLIE SNOWDON

nosy

Also by

HELEN PETERS

LOOK OUT FOR:

A Piglet Called Truffle

A Duckling Called Button

A Sheepdog Called Sky

A Kitten Called Holly

A Lamb Called Lucky

A Goat Called Willow

An Otter Called Pebble

An Owl Called Star

A Deer Called Dotty

A Donkey Called Mistletoe

A Foal Called Storm

A Puppy Called Sparkle

FOR OLDER READERS:

The Secret Hen House Theatre

The Farm Beneath the Water

Evie's Ghost

Anna at War

Chapter One
A Real Seal

On the first morning of the summer holidays, Jasmine and her best friend Tom took Jasmine's sheepdog, Sky, for a walk along the riverbank. The fields of Oak Tree Farm, Jasmine's home, stretched out ahead of them. Although they were on a public footpath, there was nobody else in sight.

"Oh, look, Tom!" said Jasmine, as they rounded a bend.

A family of swans was gliding through the water, two parents followed by six fluffy grey cygnets.

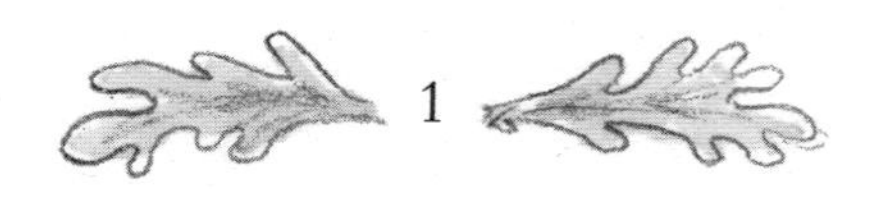

Sky strained towards them.

"No, Sky," said Jasmine, keeping a firm hold on his lead. "Leave the swans alone."

"Those cygnets are so cute," said Tom. "All swimming in a row."

They continued along the path until a movement on the opposite bank caught Jasmine's eye. Her mouth fell open in astonishment. She stopped and stared, trying to make sense of this incredible sight. Could it really be true?

Wide-eyed in amazement, she grabbed Tom's arm and pointed across the river.

Tom gasped.

Jasmine couldn't speak. She couldn't have been more surprised if she had seen a mermaid lying on the riverbank.

Stretched out on the grass, just above the mud that was exposed at low tide, lay a large seal. It had big dark eyes and long white whiskers. Its coat was grey, mottled with white, changing to

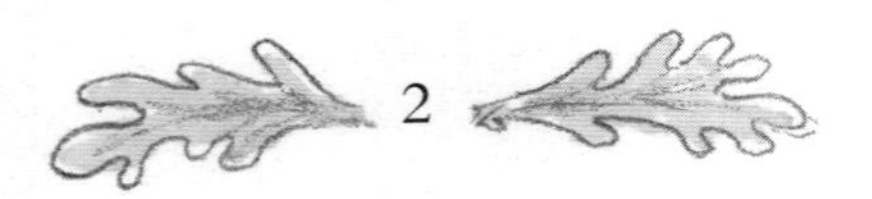

a creamy colour on its throat and front. It had long rear flippers and surprisingly small front flippers.

It was quite extraordinary to see such an exotic sea creature lounging casually on the bank. *On our farm!* thought Jasmine in wonder. *A seal on our farm!*

The children were hidden by the bushes on their side of the river, and the seal didn't seem to have noticed them. It gazed out across the fields.

Tom turned to speak, but Jasmine put her finger to her lips. Signalling to him to follow, she tiptoed back along the path, keeping a tight hold on Sky's lead. Luckily he didn't seem interested in the seal.

Once they were a safe distance away, the children turned to each other and grinned in delight.

"I can't believe it!" whispered Jasmine. "It is a seal, isn't it? A real seal?"

"It actually is," said Tom in awe. "An actual seal on your river! It must have swum up from the sea."

"Do they do that? I didn't know seals came this far away from the sea."

"Remember when we went to London Aquarium? There were pictures of seals in the River Thames, right in the middle of London. That's much further from the sea than we are."

"Wow," breathed Jasmine, peeping through the bushes. "It's so amazing."

"It's massive, isn't it?" said Tom, peering through another gap. "I didn't know seals were so big." He took his phone out of his pocket. "I'll take some photos."

"We mustn't disturb it," Jasmine said. "If it sees us, it will get frightened and leave."

"I won't go any closer. I'll use the zoom. And the sound's off."

"And we're downwind of it here," said Jasmine, "so it won't smell us."

While Tom took photos, Jasmine feasted her eyes on the seal, trying to fix every detail in her mind's eye.

The seal rolled on to its side. They watched, fascinated, as it heaved its large body around on its little front flippers. Then, as it turned away from them, Jasmine almost squealed. She clamped her hand over her mouth just in time.

"Oh!" she breathed. "A baby!"

Chapter Two
The Secret Seal Society

The mother seal turned so that she and her pup lay face to face on the riverbank, nuzzling each other's noses. The mother sniffed her pup's face and head.

"Such a gorgeous pup," whispered Jasmine.

The baby seal had enormous round dark eyes, a doggy nose and long whiskers. Its coat was much darker than its mother's, but otherwise its body was a miniature version of hers.

"It's beautiful," said Tom. "Do you think it's a newborn?"

"Maybe she came here specially to give birth," said Jasmine. "She might have wanted to be somewhere quiet."

The mother rolled on to her side again. The children watched, spellbound, as the pup found her teat and began to suckle.

After a while, Jasmine turned to Tom. "What time is it?"

Tom looked at his watch. "Nearly nine."

"I'd better call Mum and tell her we won't be back for a while. She was going to make us breakfast."

"Won't she be at work by now?"

"No, she's starting later today. Can I use your phone?"

Tom took it out of his pocket. "No signal. It's usually better higher up."

"Mum will be so excited there's a seal here," said Jasmine, as they walked up the hill away from the river. "I wonder if she's ever treated one. I bet she hasn't."

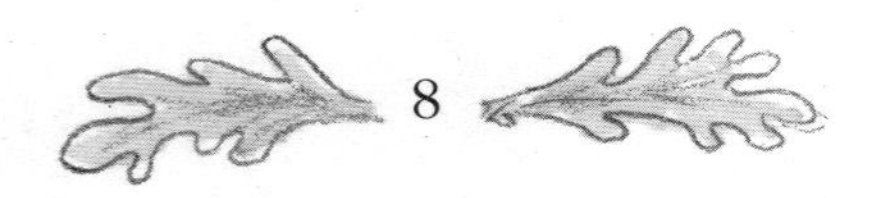

Jasmine's mum, Nadia, was a vet, and she loved encountering new and unusual animals.

"Mum, you won't believe what we've just seen on the river!" said Jasmine, when Nadia answered the phone. She told her mother all about the seal and her pup.

"Wow, that's incredible!" said Nadia. "I know they swim up rivers sometimes, but we've never had one here before. How wonderful."

"Do you want to come and see them? They're so beautiful."

"I'd love to," said Nadia, "but the less they're disturbed, the better. Seals are easily spooked when they're on land, especially mothers with pups. Don't get too close, will you, and don't let them see you."

"Of course not. We're watching from behind a bush, and we're downwind of them."

"Was there anyone else on the footpath? Any dog walkers?"

"Not at the moment."

"Good. Let's hope nobody else sees them, then. Don't tell anyone about them, will you?"

"We won't breathe a word," said Jasmine. "We'll be the Secret Seal Society."

"Perfect."

They sent Nadia some photos of the seals, and then they walked back down the hill. As they drew closer to the river, Jasmine was alarmed to hear voices. She gave Tom a fearful glance, and they quickened their pace until they reached the gap in the bushes where Jasmine had first spotted the seal.

She gasped in horror. A bright-orange kayak was pulled up on the opposite riverbank. The mother seal was nowhere to be seen. A young man and woman in wetsuits were crouching on the bank next to the baby seal. As the children stared in fury and disbelief, the woman posed with her head next to the pup's and stroked its coat, smiling for the camera as the man took photos. The pup lifted its head and gave a sad cry.

It started to wriggle along the riverbank, using its little front flippers to pull itself forward.

Boiling with rage, Jasmine wanted to yell at the couple, but that would frighten the seals even more. Instead, she waved her arms above her head to get their attention. Tom did the same.

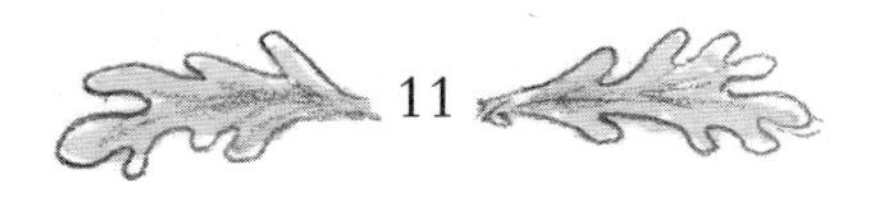

Eventually the woman noticed them.

"Hi!" she called. "Isn't this amazing? I can't believe it! Isn't it the cutest little thing?"

The man turned to the children with a grin and waved at them.

Jasmine was so angry she thought she might burst. She pressed her finger to her lips to tell them to be quiet, and then she pointed to a muddy slope further along the bank, by a weeping willow tree. She beckoned fiercely and mouthed *Come here.*

The woman frowned, looking puzzled, so Jasmine repeated the instruction.

The man raised his palms in a questioning gesture. Jasmine beckoned again.

The couple looked at each other with raised eyebrows. They obviously thought they were dealing with a lunatic, but when Jasmine beckoned them urgently for a fourth time, they shrugged and got into the kayak. The pup was still wriggling along the riverbank, looking

around in all directions and calling for its mother.

Oh, please let the mother hear and come back, thought Jasmine. The poor little pup must be terrified. Had its mum just gone out to fish, or had those stupid people scared her away? Jasmine looked at them with contempt as they paddled across the river. *If they scared her away,* she thought, *I'll kill them.*

"What's up?" asked the man, as the kayak reached the bank.

"Get out of the water," Jasmine whispered fiercely. "And stop talking."

The couple looked startled, but they got out of the kayak with some difficulty and pulled it up on to the bank.

"What's going on?" asked the woman.

"What's going on?!" hissed Jasmine. "You've just disturbed the seals, and now the mother might reject her pup! Don't you know you should never disturb wild animals?"

"Hey, calm down," said the man in a patronising tone that made Jasmine want to smack him. "The seal's fine. We barely touched it."

"Where's the mother?" Jasmine demanded. "Where did she go?"

He jerked his thumb downriver. "She went into the water when she saw us. I guess she's off hunting. Bringing some fish back for the baby."

Trembling with fury, Jasmine gave him her most withering look. "The pup isn't even weaned yet. It doesn't eat fish. All it needs is its mother's milk. So now it will starve to death if she doesn't come back."

"No need to get so upset," said the man. "What business is it of yours anyway?"

"I live on this farm," said Jasmine, "so any animal on this farm is my business. That seal had chosen this site as a safe place to have her baby, and you've just destroyed their peace. Now she might never come back, and her pup will be orphaned."

They all looked across the river at the pup, who lifted its head and gave a desolate cry that made Jasmine's heart ache.

The woman looked uncomfortable. "I'm sure the mum will be back soon," she said.

"Oh, are you? And what if she's not?"

"She will be, don't worry," said the man. "Come on, Caitlin, let's go."

"What are your names?" asked Jasmine.

The man drew back. "Listen, kid, cut the attitude, will you? You're not the seal police. We're leaving now, and the mum will be back any minute."

They got into the kayak.

"Idiots," hissed Jasmine, as they paddled off up the river. "Stupid, stupid idiots."

Chapter Three
The Poor Little Pup

The pup raised its head again and gave its desperate cry. It sounded a bit like a lamb baaing for its mother. It hauled itself a few more centimetres along the riverbank. The children moved further away, so as not to stress it even more. They stopped beside a big old oak tree that stood on its own in the field.

"The poor little pup," said Tom. "What should we do?"

Jasmine's head was filled with fury at the kayakers and pity for the seal pup. She forced

herself to calm down and think.

"I guess we should wait for the mother to come back. Maybe we should search for her. One of us could walk along the river while the other one watches the pup."

Tom frowned. "I don't see how searching would help. We can't exactly herd her back."

"No, but at least we'd know if she was close by, and we could see if she was swimming back towards the pup."

"But we might scare her further away if she saw us. I think we should just stay here and watch."

"You stay," said Jasmine. "I'll go and ask Mum what to do."

"Are you going to phone her?"

"No, I need to go home anyway. We might end up watching for hours, so I'll have to go and feed the animals first. And I'll bring some food back. I'm starving."

"I'll climb the tree," said Tom. "I should get a

good view from up there. Can you bring your dad's binoculars? Then we can get a closer look at the pup."

"Sure," said Jasmine, and she hurried across the fields to the farmhouse.

When Jasmine returned, Tom was sitting on the lowest branch of the oak tree, dangling his legs.

"You were gone for ages," he said.

Jasmine dumped a bulging rucksack on the grass. "I had a lot to do. Did the mum come back?"

"No, the pup's still there, crying. It's so sad.

What did your mum say?"

Jasmine pulled some crumpled sheets of paper from her bag and handed them up to him. "She printed these out while I was feeding the animals. I haven't read them yet. She had to go to work, but she said to call her if anything changes. She was really angry with the kayakers. Budge up."

Tom shuffled along the branch as Jasmine hoisted the rucksack back on to her shoulders and climbed up to join him. From the branch she could see the abandoned pup flopping along the riverbank, calling forlornly for its mother.

"Poor little thing," she said. "I could kill those kayakers."

She rummaged in her rucksack and took out yoghurts, spoons, bananas and KitKats. She balanced their breakfasts carefully on the broad branch, while Tom scanned through the information Nadia had printed.

"It says here," he said, "that human disturbance is one of the biggest risks to seals. They have to haul out of the water to rest and digest their food, but they can't move very well on land, so if they're disturbed, they get really stressed. Often the mothers will rush back into the water and abandon their pups. And it says the most likely time for the mother and pup to be separated is in the first two days."

"Really? Why?"

"It says after two days she can recognise her pup by its sound and smell, but before that they're not fully bonded."

"Hopefully this one is older," said Jasmine.

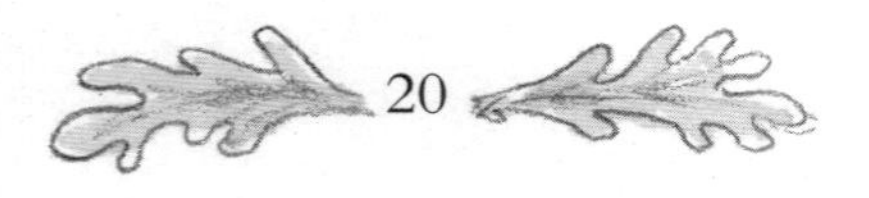

"This article says if it still has its umbilical cord attached, it's probably less than two days old."

Jasmine took her dad's binoculars out of her rucksack and focused them on the pup. "I can't see an umbilical cord, but if it's there, the pup's probably sitting on it."

Tom turned to the next sheet of paper. "*When to Worry About a Lone Seal Pup,*" he read. "There's a checklist of signs to look for."

"What are they?"

"Is it injured or bleeding?"

"It doesn't seem to be," said Jasmine, examining the pup through the binoculars. "But I can only see one side of it."

"Is it distressed or non-responsive?"

"It's definitely distressed," said Jasmine, her heart aching at the sight of the crying pup.

"Umbilical cord still attached? We're not sure. Alone for several hours or no parent visible? Well, it hasn't been alone for several hours yet."

"It seems cruel to leave it on its own for hours when it's so distressed," said Jasmine.

"But we have to, otherwise the mother won't return. It would be worse to take it away, if the mother might come back for it."

The pup rolled on to its side.

"Oh, Tom!" cried Jasmine. "It's still got its umbilical cord!"

"Really? Are you sure?"

"Yes, look." She passed him the binoculars.

"Wow," said Tom. "That means it's under two days old."

"I'll go and call Mum," said Jasmine. "If it's that young, we probably shouldn't leave it much longer."

She walked up the hill to make the phone call. Nadia said she would talk to someone she knew called Elspeth.

"She's a retired vet who trained as a Marine Mammal Medic," said Nadia. "She volunteers with the local seal rescue charity, so she'll be able to advise us. Call me back in half an hour."

Jasmine relayed this to Tom, who was reading more information.

"This article says the mother doesn't go off alone to forage for food until the pup's about ten days old," he said. "So she hasn't gone hunting. I don't think she's going to come back."

Chapter Four
Not a Job for Kids

It was almost midday, and the pup was still wandering about on the bank, crying for its mother.

"Poor little thing," said Jasmine. "Those kayakers should be sent to prison."

"I know," said Tom. "Imagine orphaning a seal pup, just to get a selfie."

"We should give it a name. Even if it's only here for a few hours."

Tom nodded. "It should be something to do with the sea. What about Seaweed?"

Jasmine wrinkled her nose. "It's much too cute to be called Seaweed."

"Ocean?"

Jasmine gazed at the pup in thought. The sunlight caught its sleek coat, making it look like a shining pearl on the muddy riverbank.

"I know! We should call it Pearl."

"That's nice," said Tom. "And pearls come from the sea."

"Exactly."

When Jasmine called her mum back, Nadia said, "How are things? Any change? Has the mother returned?"

"No. The pup's so sad; it's awful to watch."

"I spoke to Elspeth," said Nadia, "and she said if the mother hasn't returned by five o'clock, she'll come out to assess the pup."

"And then what?"

"Well, if it needs to be rescued, then I assume she'll take it to the rehabilitation centre. And before you start, Jasmine, no, you cannot keep the seal at home."

"I wouldn't keep a seal at home," said Jasmine indignantly. "Seals aren't pets."

"Well, that's very mature of you. Good." Nadia sounded surprised and relieved.

"I'd only rehabilitate it at home," said Jasmine. "Then I'd release it."

"Jasmine!"

"Why not? I'm sure we could rehabilitate it as well as anyone else."

"No," said Nadia in her sternest voice. "Absolutely not. I'm not even discussing it. I have to get back to work. Call me if anything changes."

Jasmine said goodbye and took the phone back to Tom. "Let's find out about rehabilitating seal pups," she said.

Tom looked doubtful. "It would need a pool, wouldn't it?"

"If it needs a pool, we'll find one," said Jasmine. "They'll all try to stop us, but we could

look after it as well as anybody else could, as long as we know what to do. So let's research it on your phone. We've got until five o'clock to find out everything we need to know."

They took turns to watch the river, but the mother didn't reappear. Jasmine made an emergency trip back to the farmhouse to fetch more food. The pup was still alone when she returned.

She phoned Nadia at five, and Nadia said she would call Elspeth. "I'll ask Dad to bring her to the field when she gets to the farm," she said.

Some time later, Jasmine saw her dad's truck heading in their direction. It stopped at the entrance to Hill Field and Dad got out, followed by a stern-looking older woman with short grey hair. She was wearing wellies and navy-blue overalls.

The children scrambled down the tree and walked towards the truck. The woman didn't

even glance at them. She strode to the back of the truck and took out a large plastic dog carrier.

"She looks scary," whispered Tom.

Jasmine nodded in agreement.

"Hello, kids," said Dad. "This is Elspeth, from the Marine Life Rescue. Whereabouts is the pup?"

"It's on the other side of the river, right opposite that oak tree," said Jasmine. "Crawling around on the bank. It's stopped crying; I think it's exhausted."

Dad led the way to a little wooden bridge. Elspeth followed, and Jasmine and Tom walked behind at a safe distance. Elspeth hadn't even looked at the children, and Jasmine didn't want to draw attention to their presence in case she sent them away. They hung back as the adults reached the clearing and Elspeth gave the carrier to Dad.

The little pup was lying on the bank with its eyes closed. Jasmine's stomach squirmed in dread. Were they too late?

Elspeth slowly approached the pup and crouched beside it. After a minute, she walked back to Dad.

"Yes, it definitely needs rescuing," she said. "The mother won't return, unfortunately; she'll have headed back to sea. We have to focus on ensuring the pup survives."

"Is it a boy or a girl?" asked Jasmine.

"Female," said Elspeth without looking at her. She turned her back on the children and spoke to Dad. "The problem is, I'm not sure where it can go. Our hospital's completely full, and we've called other local places, but they're full too. I might end up driving to the other end of the country."

"Oh, dear," said Dad. "Sounds like you're very busy."

"We just don't have room for all the casualties we're seeing at the moment. We're having to refer them to other organisations, or to vets when we can't find an alternative place. Seals need space and water, and we've only got facilities for a limited number."

Jasmine's heart was beating fast. "What about us?"

Elspeth shot her a scornful look. "You?"

"Yes. We've got the space, and we've rescued lots of animals. We could look after Pearl."

Elspeth snorted in contempt and turned back to Dad. "And there you see our problem. People see a seal pup and they think, because it looks cute and cuddly, they can treat it like a toy. And it's that sort of ignorant attitude that makes our job ten times more difficult. You can't just pick up a seal pup and take it home like a stray kitten. It needs specialist facilities and specialist care. It's not a job for kids."

Jasmine glared at Elspeth. How dare she talk to her like that! Clearly she was going to have to put this woman straight on a few things.

Chapter Five
A Serious Offer

"I wouldn't call Jasmine ignorant," Dad said to Elspeth. "She's very good at looking after animals."

Jasmine drew herself up as tall as she could. "Tom and I are experienced animal rescuers. And we've found out all about rehabilitating seal pups."

"This is a serious situation, not a game," snapped Elspeth. "So please stop wasting my time."

"I'm not. I'm making a serious offer."

"I've already told you: this isn't a job for amateurs. Seal pups need a specialist diet for a start."

"I know. A liquid diet based on a multi-milk formula, with fish oil and digestive enzymes to help weight gain, plus a small amount of fish such as mackerel or herring blended with it, given five times a day."

Elspeth's mouth opened slightly.

Dad grinned. "These two always do their research."

"Mum can get all the stuff we need," said Jasmine, "and if the pup won't take a bottle, she and Dad can do tube feeding."

Feeding a baby animal through a stomach tube was a skilled job, and one that Jasmine was happy to leave to her parents. Nadia and Michael had tube-fed a lot of animals, and they could do it so that it caused the animal no distress or discomfort.

"They also need an outdoor pen with a bath or pool," said Elspeth. "And a covered sleeping area."

“We’ve got an empty dog kennel with an outdoor pen,” said Jasmine. “It’s bigger than the ones in the seal hospital. We looked at the pictures.”

“I’m sure I could get hold of a bath,” said Dad. “I can phone the local scrap dealer.”

Jasmine stared at him in astonishment.

“It’s far too much of a commitment,” said Elspeth. “Three or four months of intensive care.”

“Not if we use the fast-track method,” said Jasmine.

Elspeth’s eyebrows shot up in surprise.

“What’s the fast-track method?” asked Dad.

“It’s a way of rehabilitating seal pups that’s more like the way they’re weaned in nature,” said Jasmine.

"A lot of rescued pups are kept for months after weaning and trained to eat dead fish, but in the fast-track method they're just fed a really rich liquid formula and released after about forty days, when they've reached the same weaning weight as wild pups."

"In the wild the pup drinks the mother's milk for three to six weeks," said Tom. "The milk's really fatty, so the pup doubles its birth weight in that time. And after the pup's weaned, the mother goes off and takes no more interest in it, and the pup starts foraging for fish. Well, they mostly eat shrimp and bottom-dwelling crustaceans for the first couple of weeks, then they move on to fish."

"The pups in the trial we read about were tagged before they were released," said Jasmine, "and they all survived and learned to forage for fish."

"Interesting," said Dad.

"There are so many different opinions around

the best methods to use," said Elspeth, turning her back on the children and talking only to Michael. "All the rescue organisations have the same goal, which is to release the seal back into its natural habitat so it can live successfully in the wild. But there are lots of different ideas about the best ways to do that. I think the fast-track method makes a lot of sense actually. I've been suggesting for a while that we should try it at the hospital."

"So can we do it?" asked Jasmine. "Can we rehabilitate the pup ourselves?"

"It's not that easy," said Elspeth. "You'd need to spend several hours a day caring for it, feeding it, preparing the food, cleaning out the pen. It's a lot of work."

"We've looked after lots of animals," said Jasmine. "We know how much time it takes."

"Orphaned seal pups are very vulnerable," Elspeth said to Michael. "Especially when they're first rescued."

"That's why we don't want Pearl to have a long car journey," said Jasmine. "We can put her straight in the kennel."

"What state is the kennel in?" Elspeth asked Dad.

"It's in good condition," he said, "and it's been cleaned out, but it will need a bit of a spruce-up."

"We can go and disinfect it now," said Jasmine.

"What about the flooring?" asked Elspeth, still speaking only to Dad.

"Brick," he said. "Probably not good for a seal, I'm guessing. I could put down some plastic sheeting."

"That would be better."

"And would it need the bath immediately?" he asked. "I might not be able to get hold of one today."

"That's fine. Seals are only semi-aquatic. They spend a lot of time out of the water."

"Shall we go and clean the kennel?" asked Jasmine.

"Wait a minute," said Dad, pulling his phone from his pocket. "I need to check with Mum."

"Why?"

"Because she'll have to do a lot of the work, and you can't just bring a seal pup home without asking her."

But Dad had no signal on his phone either.

"Mum said she was going to be in surgery," said Jasmine. "So she wouldn't be able to answer anyway. And we can't wait until she's out of surgery. The pup needs help straight away."

Dad gave a weary smile. "As you can see, Elspeth, Jasmine is very strong-minded. And she and Tom have an impressive animal-rescue record. They've looked after everything from a duck egg to a donkey."

He paused. Jasmine held her breath.

"Why not?" said Dad. "Let's take on the seal pup. I'm sure Nadia would agree."

"Thank you, Dad!" said Jasmine, as she and Tom grinned at each other in delight.

"Thank you, Michael," said Elspeth. "I'm sure you and Nadia will do an excellent job."

Jasmine and Tom exchanged indignant looks.

"And obviously you can call me whenever you need help or advice," said Elspeth. "Can you give me a hand to get her in the crate?"

From the carrier she took a towel, a cloth sack and two pairs of thick gloves. She handed a pair to Dad.

"In case she bites," she said. "Even young pups can give a nasty bite."

"The pups in the fast-track method became completely tame to handle and feed," said Jasmine. "They really liked human company."

"Isn't that a problem when they go back into the wild?" asked Dad.

"The researchers thought it might be, but it wasn't. They said only one pup wanted to approach humans after being released, and even then it didn't have any bad effects."

"I'll be interested to see how you get on with the fast-track method," Elspeth said to Dad. "It will be a very helpful comparison to what most rescue centres – including us – do."

"We'll go and disinfect the kennel," said Jasmine. "Then Pearl can settle in as soon as possible."

Chapter Six
What Have You Done?

The large brick kennel stood between the farmhouse and the orchard. Its back door led to the orchard and its front door opened into a wire-fenced pen by the front of the house.

Jasmine's pet pig, Truffle, used to sleep in the kennel, but when Dotty, her deer, had come to live at the farm, Dad had built a shelter in the orchard. Then Mistletoe the donkey had joined them, and now they all shared the shelter. Sometimes Jasmine's tame duck, Button, would come and visit too. He was there now, drinking

from the water trough.

When Dad and Elspeth arrived, they left Pearl's crate in the van until her new home was ready. Dad covered the floors of the kennel and the run with tarpaulin, and Tom and Jasmine fetched logs from the woodshed to hold it down at the sides.

"It's lucky Manu's sleeping over at Ben's tonight," said Jasmine, as they wheeled a barrow full of logs to the pen. "At least Pearl will have a bit of peace while she settles in."

"Yes," Tom agreed. Jasmine's little brother wasn't exactly a peaceful kind of person.

When Elspeth had pronounced the accommodation satisfactory (still completely ignoring the children), they stood outside while she set Pearl's crate in the pen, lifted the towel away at one end and opened the crate door. The pup looked out and gave a desolate call.

"Hello, Pearl," whispered Jasmine. "Welcome to your new home."

Elspeth drove back to the wildlife hospital to fetch the food and equipment they would need for the first few days, while Jasmine, Tom and Dad watched Pearl from outside the pen. She lifted her head and peered round the side of the crate.

“She’s so cute,” said Jasmine. “Such enormous eyes.”

Pearl turned her head from side to side, inspecting her new surroundings. Then, propelling herself on her front flippers, she wriggled out of the crate. She stayed still for a minute, looking around her, and then she lolloped across the floor towards the children. She looked directly at them and gave a plaintive cry.

“She’s asking us for help,” said Tom.

“She’s probably hungry,” said Jasmine. “I hope

she'll drink from a bottle. How amazing to bottle-feed a seal pup."

"Poor little thing," said Dad. "All on her own like that."

"She looks as though she wants to make friends with us," said Jasmine. "I'm sure she'll be tame really soon, and then we can play with her and keep her company."

"We won't be there at night, though," said Tom. "We should give her a soft toy to cuddle up with. I know it's not the same as having her mum, but it's better than nothing."

"What about Flipper? You know, my cuddly dolphin. He's quite big, and he's the same sort of shape as a seal."

"He'll get ruined."

"That's OK. Pearl needs a friend."

"Good idea," said Dad. "Definitely gets my seal of approval."

"Oh, very funny," said Jasmine.

Dad grinned. "Shall I bring it down? I'm going upstairs before I head out to the calves."

"Yes, please," said Jasmine.

As Dad headed inside, Tom said, "He seems really keen, doesn't he?"

"I know. I think he's quite excited."

Then she heard a sound that made her stomach squirm. "Uh-oh, that's Mum's car. She's going to be so mad."

Tom looked pale and tense.

"Don't worry," Jasmine reassured him. "She'll be mad with me, not you."

This didn't make Tom look any more relaxed.

Nadia appeared at the garden gate and smiled at the children. Then she saw Pearl. She stared at Jasmine, her expression a mixture of fury and disbelief.

"What have you done?"

"It was an emergency. They didn't have any room at the seal hospital, and—"

Mum held up a hand for silence. Her face was tight with anger.

"I can't believe you did this without asking me. I *told* you I wouldn't allow it."

"We tried to ask you. We phoned, but you didn't answer."

"Because I was working! This is completely unacceptable, Jasmine. I said—"

"Here we are!" called Dad.

They turned to see him standing in the

doorway, holding the dolphin toy in front of his face.

"Pearl, meet Flipper, your new friend," he said.

Silence.

Dad lowered the toy and saw Mum glaring at him.

"Oh, hi, Nadia."

"So you were in on this, too," she said.

"I did try to call you."

"So I heard."

The pup gave a despairing cry. Nadia turned towards her. "Oh, you poor little thing. What happened to your mum?"

"She came straight up to us," Jasmine said. "She's really friendly. Or maybe she's just hungry. Hopefully she'll take a bottle, but if not, we'll have to tube-feed her."

"Oh, will we?" said Nadia. "And who will be the person doing that, I wonder?"

"I'll share it with you," said Dad. "I'll do as many feeds as I can. And Jasmine will make up the formula and do everything else, won't you, Jas?"

"Of course," said Jasmine. "And Tom will come every day."

"How will you have time to look after a seal as well as all your other animals?" said Nadia.

"We'll find the time. It's the holidays anyway. Or would you rather I sat in front of a screen all summer?"

"Of course not, but—"

"So you should be pleased that I want to look after animals. And it's not like we wanted this to happen; it was those stupid people who scared her mum away. And the seal hospital doesn't have space for her. She might have had to go hundreds of miles away, and she was already in distress."

Pearl looked up at Nadia and gave another plaintive cry.

Nadia looked at her and her face softened. She crouched down beside the pen. "You're gorgeous, aren't you?"

"We're going to use this fast-track method we've read about," said Jasmine. "It's more like the way seals are weaned in the wild, and it takes less than forty days, so she'll be released by the end of the holidays."

"You've worked it all out, haven't you?"

"Yes. And Elspeth's bringing food and

equipment. And Dad's going to get a bath for her."

Nadia gave Michael a steely look. "Is he, indeed?"

Dad shrugged. "A seal needs water."

Nadia turned back to Jasmine and sighed. "Well, I suppose I should be grateful that you're planning to release her at least."

"Of course!" said Jasmine. "She's a sea creature. She needs to be in the sea."

Nadia looked at Pearl for a long time. "All right, then," she said eventually. "Since she's here, let's rehabilitate her as well as we possibly can, and make sure she has a successful release. I'm sure we'll learn a lot on the way."

"Oh, thank you, Mum!" said Jasmine. "Thank you so much!"

Chapter Seven
Sardine Milkshake

When Elspeth returned with a large box of supplies, she seemed relieved to see Nadia. "Here's the seal milk recipe," she said.

Jasmine held out her hand to take the piece of paper. Elspeth ignored her and handed it to Nadia. As Elspeth bent down to take something else from the box, Jasmine mouthed to her mother, "She hates me."

Nadia smiled and handed Jasmine the recipe.

Elspeth stood up, her arms full of boxes and tubs. "Can I put these in your kitchen? And I'll

make up the first batch of formula if that would help."

"What would really help," said Nadia, "is if you could show Jasmine and Tom how to do it. They'll be in charge of that."

Elspeth gave the children a withering glance and turned back to Mum. "Are you sure? It's vital to get the formula right."

"They're very responsible," said Nadia. "And they've successfully rehabilitated several animals."

"Hm," said Elspeth, tight-lipped. She followed the children into the kitchen.

While Elspeth watched them disapprovingly, Tom and Jasmine measured out the milk powder and tipped it into the blender. They added half a tin of sardines and enough warm water to make it up to a litre. Then they blended it to a smooth milk. Elspeth swirled the mixture around to check for lumps and seemed disappointed not to find any. She handed them a baby's bottle.

"I've cut a cross in the teat to make the hole big enough. Start with two hundred millilitres at each feed and gradually increase it. You can keep the rest in the fridge. I'll give you a chart with the recommended quantities. Wait," she said to Jasmine, who was about to start pouring the milk in. "First you put the fish oil in the bottle. Just to the ten-millilitre mark. Then pour in the milk to make it up to two hundred millilitres and stir it thoroughly."

"Sardine milkshake. Yum," said Jasmine.

"We should give a glass to Manu," said Tom. "He'd probably love it."

"True," said Jasmine. "He eats anything."

"That would be extremely irresponsible," said Elspeth.

Jasmine shot a glance at Tom. Elspeth clearly wasn't a person to joke with.

"Always heat the milk to lukewarm before you feed her," Elspeth said.

"Body temperature, like for a lamb?" asked Jasmine.

"Exactly. And just before feeding, stir in half of one of these enzyme capsules. The enzymes make the milk more digestible for seals, so adding them will help her gain weight."

"Shall we feed her now?" asked Tom.

"She needs rehydrating first, so I'm going to make a dilute milk for that. She's very unlikely to take a bottle, so your parents will need to tube-feed her."

Oh, you'd love that, wouldn't you? thought Jasmine.

"I need to weigh her before feeding. Do you have bathroom scales?"

"I'll get them," Jasmine said. She pictured the little seal flopping over the edges of the scales. "How will we put her on them?"

"I'll use the box I brought the food in."

When they took the scales outside, Pearl was at the edge of the pen, sniffing Nadia's shoes through the wire.

"You'll need to weigh her every day," said Elspeth. "Weight gain is the most important indicator of her health. We're aiming for her to gain weight at the same rate as a seal fed by its mother."

"I'll make a chart and fill it in every day," said Tom.

Nadia smiled. "Tom's an excellent record-keeper."

Elspeth ignored this. "She should gain at

least a quarter of a kilo a day, hopefully more. Contact me straight away if she isn't putting on weight, or if you're concerned about anything else, Nadia."

She pulled on her thick gloves and took the box and scales into the pen. She set the box on the scales, grabbed Pearl firmly round the middle and put her in the box.

"She's nine point two kilos. Small for her age. We need her to get to twenty kilos before we release her."

She took Pearl out of the box and asked Nadia to straddle her on the ground while she took the pup's temperature and checked for signs of illness or injury. When she was satisfied that Pearl didn't need medical attention, she went indoors to make up the rehydration formula.

"Can I try feeding her?" asked Jasmine, when Elspeth brought the bottle out. "Please?"

"She's very unlikely to take it," said Elspeth, "and she might bite."

"I don't mind."

"Just wear the gloves," said Nadia.

Jasmine put on the huge gloves and stepped into the pen. The little seal fixed her enormous eyes on her. Jasmine held out the bottle. Pearl sniffed it tentatively. Then she sniffed the gloves. Everyone watched in silence.

Jasmine held the teat against the pup's mouth and squeezed until a little milk dribbled on to Pearl's lips. This often worked with lambs, helping them realise what the bottle contained.

The pup kept her face still, as though considering the idea. Jasmine offered her the teat again. This time Pearl raised her head, took the teat in her mouth, and started to suck.

Jasmine beamed at her, but she didn't say anything in case she distracted Pearl from feeding.

After a few seconds, Pearl pulled away from the bottle. Jasmine offered it to her again, and again she drank. When almost all the milk had gone, the pup pulled away. Jasmine offered her the bottle back, but she wouldn't open her mouth.

"Well done, Pearl," Jasmine murmured, stroking her sleek dark fur. "You did so well."

"It probably won't last," said Elspeth. "She might reject the bottle at any time and need to be tube-fed."

"So I'll feed her again around midnight, is that right?" said Nadia.

"I can do that," said Jasmine.

"No, you can't," Nadia said. "You can do all the other feeds, though."

"Give the first morning feed around eight," said Elspeth, "and then every four hours until midnight. I've brought a trampoline for her to sleep on, too."

"A trampoline?" said Nadia.

"One of those little exercise trampolines. Pups seem to love sleeping on them."

She and Nadia went out to her car, and Jasmine and Tom were left alone with Pearl. Tom came into the pen and placed the toy dolphin next to the pup. She ignored it and started sucking on Tom's trousers.

He laughed. "She definitely likes company. She must be missing her mum so much."

"It's sad that she'll be on her own all night," said Jasmine. "Flipper's not really the same as a live friend."

Then she drew in her breath and looked at Tom.

"What?" said Tom. "You're not going to smuggle her indoors, are you?"

"Of course not! But I read an article on your phone about how pups are happier and healthier if they're kept in pairs. They said when a second pup was introduced, they spent all their time together, like a pup would with its mother. Even when they were released, they followed each other out to sea."

"That's so cute," said Tom.

"So that shows how much seal pups need company. They're supposed to be with their mum until they're weaned, and poor Pearl lost her mum after only two days. She needs a seal friend while she grows up. So we should get another pup."

Tom's eyebrows shot up. "What? How?"

"Easy. We ask Elspeth. Her hospital's full, so if she has to rescue another pup, we can ask her to bring it here, to keep Pearl company."

"But she hates us."

"She doesn't hate Mum and Dad. So if they sent her an email…"

"But they won't want another pup."

"No, but if I sent an email from Mum's computer..."

"Pretending it's from your mum? She'd go crazy."

"I wouldn't actually pretend. She often doesn't sign her name on emails; she just writes a quick message. So I wouldn't actually be pretending to be her. Elspeth would just *assume* it was from her. It's not my fault if she assumes things, is it?"

"What happens when Elspeth replies, though? Your mum will see the email and know what you've done."

Jasmine thought for a moment. "We'll say, we know you're busy so don't bother to reply to the email. We'll ask her to call instead. And we'll give her your number."

Chapter Eight
Pearl's First Swim

When Jasmine went to feed Pearl at eight o'clock the following morning, the little pup was lying on her side on the trampoline, snuggled up against the toy dolphin. Her head was resting on Flipper's neck and one of her front flippers lay across its back.

"Oh, Pearl," said Jasmine. "You're so gorgeous."

At the sound of her voice Pearl lifted her head, gave a cry and lolloped into the pen, propelling herself along on her little front flippers. She started to suck on Jasmine's trousers.

"You're hungry, aren't you?" said Jasmine. "Here you are."

Judging by the speed at which she drank, Pearl certainly was hungry. After she had finished, Jasmine sat in the pen and the pup cuddled up against her legs, while Jasmine stroked her silky fur.

When Mum called her in for breakfast, she kissed Pearl's head.

"I wish I could stay with you all day, but I have to go and eat, and then I need to look after Mistletoe and Dotty and Truffle. But Tom's coming after breakfast, and I'll see you again when I've done the other animals."

In the kitchen Mum was standing over a frying pan at the stove.

"Ooh, pancakes!" said Jasmine.

"Well, it's the holidays." She turned and saw the empty bottle in Jasmine's hand. "Oh, great, she drank the whole lot. It's fantastic that she's taking a bottle. So much easier

than tube feeding, and it must be nicer for her, too. More like suckling from her mother."

"She really likes company, doesn't she?" said Jasmine. "Wouldn't it be good if she had another seal pup with her?"

Mum laughed. "Are you planning to set up a seal sanctuary now?"

Jasmine was about to tell her she wasn't joking, but then she thought better of it. She would plant the seed gradually.

As she finished her last pancake, the kitchen door was flung open and Manu burst in, followed by his best friend, Ben.

"There's a seal in the kennel!" said Manu. "Where did it come from? Are we keeping it?"

"Ah, you've seen her," said Mum. "Hello, Ben."

"Hello, Nadia. How are you today?"

Ben was always really polite to adults. It was how he got away with being so naughty.

"Is it really an actual seal?" asked Manu

"Yes," said Jasmine. "Her name's Pearl and I'm rehabilitating her. And you two have to stay away, OK? She needs peace and quiet."

"She doesn't have anything to swim in," said Manu. "Where's she going to swim?"

"Dad's collecting a bath," said Nadia. "From the scrap-metal dealer."

"Is he fetching it now?" asked Jasmine. "I can't wait to see her swimming."

"Can me and Ben go in the bath with her?" asked Manu, jumping up and down with excitement. "I've always wanted to swim with a seal."

Jasmine threw up her hands in exasperation. "Didn't you hear what I just said? She needs peace and quiet, not two idiot boys frightening her to death."

Manu opened his mouth to retort, but the back-door latch rattled, and Dad called, "Is anyone up for a bit of digging?"

"Me!" said Manu. "We are, aren't we, Ben?"

"Digging what?" asked Jasmine, as Dad appeared in the kitchen doorway.

"Well, I went to collect the bath," said Dad, "but when I told Dave what it was for, he said his neighbour was getting rid of a plastic pond."

"A pond? How big?"

"Come and have a look. It's in the orchard."

The children hurried out after him. In the orchard, next to the back door of Pearl's kennel, lay a moulded black plastic pond. The middle was quite deep, but it had ledges like steps that made it shallower towards the sides. Mistletoe stood beside it, sniffing it curiously.

"Pearl will love it," said Jasmine. "Thanks so much, Dad."

"I was a bit worried about how she'd get in and out of a bath," said Dad, "so I think this is better. We'll sink it into the ground so she can slip straight in, and she'll be able to haul herself out using the ledges."

"We'll need to dig a massive hole," said Manu delightedly. "Come on, Ben, let's get spades."

Dad smiled as the boys ran off towards the garden shed. "I think they're going to find it tougher than they imagine, getting through this ground."

"Will Pearl be OK out here?" asked Jasmine, looking at the enormous pig flopped on her side in the grass. "What if she's frightened of Truffle?"

"Don't worry, I'll fence it off. Seal off the area."

Jasmine groaned. "Dad! No more seal jokes."

"Sorry. But it will be good to have the pool enclosed. Then, when she's a bit older, you can

keep the back door of the kennel open, and she can go in the water whenever she wants."

Jasmine looked at her dad. He didn't usually throw himself into her animal-rescue projects like this. Normally she had to ask for his help.

"Thanks, Dad," she said.

"Well, it's not every day we get to have a seal pup living at the farm. It's pretty special."

And Jasmine remembered how, when they had visited Norfolk a few years ago, he had been just as excited as she was to see the huge colony of seals hauled out on the beach.

With Dad's help loosening the earth, and everyone helping to dig, the hole was eventually deep enough for the pond. Mum came out to see how they were getting on.

"Oh, my goodness," she said to the boys. "You appear to be wearing mostly soil. I'm going to have to hose you down."

"We dug up loads of Roman pottery, look," said Manu.

Jasmine peered at the muddy fragments. "Looks like broken bits of flowerpot to me."

"That shows how much you know. They're probably from a mosaic, like that one on the school trip. I bet there's a whole Roman villa under this orchard."

Dad fenced off the area with chicken wire and Jasmine brought the hose across to fill the pond. Manu begged to do it, but Dad said, "Not after the last time I let you use the hose. You practically turned the garden into a lake."

When the pond was full, everyone gathered in the orchard to watch Pearl's first swim. Jasmine opened the back door of the kennel, and the pup shimmied to the door and sniffed the air.

"Look, Pearl," said Jasmine, crouching down and rippling the water with her fingers. "This is for you."

Pearl shuffled to the edge of the pond. She dipped her whiskers in the water and sniffed. Then she turned to Jasmine, as if for explanation.

"It's for you, Pearl," said Jasmine. "To swim in."

Pearl sniffed the water again and turned back to Jasmine.

"Take your time," said Jasmine. "There's no hurry."

"Maybe she doesn't like swimming," said Manu. "Maybe she's the only seal in the world who's afraid of water."

"Perhaps she doesn't want to go in on her own," said Tom. "If she was in the wild, her mum would take her in."

"I'll go in with her!" said Manu. "I can pretend to be her mum!"

"No need to fuss," said Dad. "She'll go in when she's ready."

And, as he said this, the little pup placed her front flippers in the water and slipped under the surface.

Manu and Ben laughed in excitement, while Jasmine and Tom beamed like proud parents.

"Wow, she can swim underwater already!" Ben exclaimed.

"Two-day-old pups can stay underwater for two minutes," said Tom. "I was reading about it last night. Their ear openings close when they dive, like built-in earplugs. They slow down their heartbeat too, to save oxygen. When seals do deep dives, they can stay underwater for half an hour, and they slow their heartbeat down to three or four beats a minute."

"Wow," said Dad. "I had no idea."

"They can sleep in the water, too," said Jasmine. "They just leave their heads out. It's so cute."

Pearl raised her head and gave a little call. She paddled back to the side of the pond and nosed around, flailing her front flippers, before planting them on the edge and hauling herself out.

"Didn't she like it?" asked Manu. "She only stayed in a few seconds."

"They don't spend long in the water at this age," said Jasmine, stroking the pup, who was sniffing her shoe.

As if to prove her wrong, Pearl shuffled back to the pond and dipped her whiskers in. Then she placed her front flippers in the water and dived in.

"Oh, she does like it!" said Manu. "She's not afraid of water after all."

"I bet she'd like it even more if she had a friend to play with," said Jasmine, and she gave Tom a meaningful look.

Chapter Nine
Appalling Behaviour

The following morning, Tom and Jasmine were mucking out Mistletoe's shelter when Tom's phone rang. He looked at the number and passed the phone to Jasmine.

"It might be Elspeth," he said. "Put it on speakerphone."

It was Elspeth, and of course she immediately asked to speak to Nadia.

"She's at work," said Jasmine with some satisfaction. "Can I take a message?"

"Can you tell her we've got another pup for her?"

"Oh, that's great!"

"It's not great at all. It's yet another example of human idiocy. Abandoned on a beach after some picnickers went too close and scared the mother away. We've had volunteers monitoring it from a distance overnight in case she returned, but there's been no sign of her."

"Oh, the poor pup."

"It's happening all the time. More people are using the beaches, and they're not properly educated about seals. Keep your distance and keep dogs on leads. It should be common sense, but clearly people need to have it spelled out for them."

"Yes," agreed Jasmine.

"So we're off to collect the pup now. Can you tell your parents I'll be there shortly?"

"Sure," said Jasmine.

She handed the phone back to Tom. He looked worried. "We're going to be in so much trouble."

"Well, we would have told her, but we can't phone when she's on an emergency call. Anyway, it's probably better this way. Once the pup's here, she can't send it back."

"There's nowhere for it to go anyway," said Tom. "The seal hospital's full."

"Exactly. Let's go and tell Pearl."

Pearl was lying on her side on the trampoline, with one flipper laid across the toy dolphin's back.

"Guess what, Pearl?" said Jasmine, as the little seal fixed her enormous eyes on her. "You're going to have a new friend to keep you company. Another seal pup. Isn't that great?"

"Seal poo smells worse than dog poo," said Tom, wrinkling his nose.

"Let's clean out the kennel," said Jasmine. "I'll bring the barrow round."

When she returned with the wheelbarrow and scoop, Tom said, "You know what Elspeth said? About telling people to leave seals alone?"

"Yes."

"And how they need to get the message across more strongly?"

"Yes."

"Well, how about if we asked the local TV station to do a story on the seals? You know, TV South?"

Jasmine's eyes widened. "You mean ask them to come here? To film the seals?"

"I bet they would. They often do stories about animals."

"They'd have to film from a distance," Jasmine said, "and not stress the seals. I bet Elspeth wouldn't allow it."

"But it would be to educate people about leaving wild seals alone, wouldn't it? TV would get the message across better than anything."

"True. And it's us who's looking after them, on our farm. It's nothing to do with Elspeth."

Mum still wasn't home when Elspeth arrived, and there was no sign of Dad either. Elspeth clearly wasn't happy about this, but there wasn't much she could do about it. She peered into the kennel to see Pearl.

"What do you think?" asked Jasmine. "Does she look well?"

"Very well," Elspeth said, and Jasmine swelled with pride.

"Can we see the new pup?" she asked.

"He's in the van."

"It's a boy?"

"Yes. A few days older than Pearl, we think. We've weighed him and checked him, and rehydrated him by tube, so he'll be fine until Pearl's next feed, and then you can feed them together. You can try him with a bottle, but he'll probably reject it. Pearl was very unusual to take to a bottle."

"I'm sure he will, too," said Jasmine.

Elspeth opened the back of the van. A beautiful seal pup with huge shining dark eyes looked out at them through the bars of a crate.

He opened his mouth and gave a cry that sounded almost like a child's.

"Hello, little boy," murmured Jasmine. "I'm so sorry you lost your mum. Stupid tourists with their stupid selfies. But you're going to meet a new friend now. She's called Pearl and she'll be your foster sister."

“Does he have a name?” Tom asked Elspeth.

“Not yet.”

“What about Silver?” said Tom. “His fur’s a sort of silvery colour, and Pearl and Silver sound good together, don’t they?”

“Perfect,” said Jasmine.

“I was reading more about harbour seals last night,” said Tom, as Elspeth carried the crate into the pen. “Did you know that every single harbour seal has a different pattern of spots on its coat? So their coats are unique, like our fingerprints.”

“Oh, good,” said Elspeth, glancing at the farm track. “Nadia’s back.”

Jasmine’s stomach lurched.

The car pulled into the yard and the engine stopped. Elspeth was crouched in front of the crate. Jasmine flattened herself against the wire door of the pen, trying to block Elspeth and the crate from view. A scared-looking Tom placed himself next to her, puffing his chest out to

make his body as wide as possible.

Nadia appeared, carrying bulging shopping bags in both hands. "Is that Elspeth's van?" she asked Jasmine. "Is Pearl OK?"

Elspeth stood up. "Hello, Nadia. Yes, Pearl looks very well. I've just delivered the new seal."

Nadia looked utterly confused. "The new…?"

"It's so good of you to take on another pup. I really appreciate…"

She tailed off as she registered Nadia's expression. Nadia fixed furious eyes on her daughter. Jasmine looked down at her wellies. Elspeth looked from Nadia to Jasmine and back again.

"You didn't know about this?"

"No," said Nadia shortly.

"But you emailed me to say you'd be happy to take on another pup, to keep Pearl company."

"*I* emailed you?"

Elspeth stared at the children, her cheeks reddening. Jasmine's toes curled. Every muscle in her body was tense.

"I didn't sign your name on the email." Her throat was tight, and her voice sounded strange.

"But you sent a message from my email address to say we'd be happy to take on another pup." Nadia's tone was icy.

"I said we'd be happy with it because I was sure you would be," Jasmine hurried on. "The thing is, if you think about it, having two seals will actually be easier than one. They'll keep each other company, and they'll be happier and healthier. They're used to being in pairs, you see, as a mother and pup, so this is much more like how they'd live in the wild. And then they can be released together as well. So you see—"

Mum held her hand up for silence. "That's enough, Jasmine."

"I'm so sorry, Nadia," said Elspeth. "I should have checked with you. It never occurred to me that a child had sent the email."

"No," said Nadia. "Why would it?"

"We were going to tell you," said Jasmine. "When Elspeth phoned this morning. But you weren't here, so we didn't get the chance."

"Well, I'll just have to take the pup away, then," said Elspeth, glaring at Jasmine. "As if he hasn't been through enough trauma already. Your parents assured me you were responsible. Clearly that was far from the truth."

Nadia frowned and opened her mouth to say something, but Tom said, "Look!"

Everybody looked. Pearl had shuffled over to the crate, and she and Silver were sniffing each other's faces through the wire door.

"Oh!" said Jasmine. "They're bonding!"

Elspeth picked up the crate. Pearl raised her

head to look at Silver.

"Couldn't we just see how they get on together?" begged Jasmine. "Please, Mum? Just to see if they bond? I'm really sorry about not asking you, but I'm sure it would be better for the pups to be together. And if they don't bond, we can send Silver away again."

Nadia was silent for a horribly long time. Elspeth put the crate down.

Finally Mum said, "I don't actually object to having a second pup. In fact, if you'd asked, I would have said yes. I completely agree that it's better for Pearl to have a companion. It's better for most animals to have a companion. But it was appalling behaviour to go behind my back and to deceive Elspeth. That was completely irresponsible."

"I know. I'm really sorry. I don't know why I did it."

"Yes, you do. You know exactly why you did it. You were worried I'd say no. So you thought you'd go behind my back and rely on me being soft-hearted when I saw the pup. Isn't that right?"

Jasmine squirmed. "I guess."

"You don't guess. You know. But that's a very unfair way to behave, Jasmine. It puts me in a horrible position. And it's dishonest."

"I'm so sorry."

"Sorry isn't really good enough, is it? It's easy to say sorry."

"So what should I do?"

"I think you should have a think about that. But first you should apologise to Elspeth, because you've put her in a very difficult position, too."

"I'm really sorry, Elspeth," said Jasmine, her cheeks hot with shame.

Elspeth gave her a withering look.

"I'm extremely sorry, Elspeth, that Jasmine's made everything so difficult," said Nadia. "But I'm happy to take the pup."

Jasmine opened her mouth to speak, but Nadia silenced her with a gesture. "These pups will be released before the end of the summer holidays, is that right?"

"That's the plan, yes," said Elspeth. "As long as they stay healthy and keep putting on weight."

"Then that will be a lovely holiday job for Jasmine and Tom, and it will be wonderful if we can save two seal pups and give them

a successful release. But that is it, do you understand, Jasmine? I'm not prepared to get home from work and find three seal pups in the kennel. We're not taking on any more."

Jasmine nodded vigorously. "Yes, Mum. Thank you so much. I understand, I promise."

Chapter Ten
Don't Tell Manu

Mum went indoors to unpack the shopping. Pearl and Silver were still sniffing each other through the wire door of the crate. Jasmine and Tom sat outside the pen to watch as Elspeth opened the crate and left the pen.

Silver shuffled out of the crate. He and Pearl sniffed and nuzzled each other.

"They're checking each other out," whispered Tom.

After a few minutes, Pearl lolloped into the kennel. Silver followed her. Pearl rolled on to

her back and Silver reared up and flopped on top of her. They began to play-fight, rolling over and patting each other with their flippers. Jasmine and Tom laughed in delight.

"They're just like puppies, aren't they?" said Jasmine.

Pearl opened her mouth as though she was going to bite. Jasmine exclaimed in alarm, but Elspeth said, "They won't hurt each other. That's part of the play-fighting."

Sure enough, the pups rolled around together, wrestling, patting each other with their flippers and snapping their teeth but never hurting each other.

"Do you want to open the door to the pool?" asked Elspeth. "They might like to play in the water."

Strangely, since Mum had allowed Silver to stay, Elspeth seemed less hostile towards the children. Jasmine didn't understand it, but she was very relieved.

She tiptoed through the kennel so as not to disturb the pups, though they were so absorbed in their play that they took no notice of her. She opened the door to the pond enclosure and tiptoed back out.

As light flooded into the kennel from the open door, the pups stopped wrestling, raised their heads, looked around and sniffed the air. Pearl lolloped to the doorway. She sniffed the air again, then shimmied outside on to the grass. At the edge of the pond she dipped her whiskers in the water. Then she looked back at Silver and gave a little cry, as though she was calling him. Silver looked at her, hesitated for a moment and then shimmied to the edge of the pool beside her.

Pearl lowered her front flippers into the water and heaved herself in. Silver followed. Pearl dived and rolled on to her back. The pups started playing, weaving over and under each other. The children watched, entranced.

“They’re so graceful in the water,” said Jasmine. “It’s like they’re dancing.”

“They’re completely streamlined, aren’t they?” said Elspeth. “So lovely to watch.”

“Can we leave the door open all the time? I mean, not at night, but in the daytime?”

“Yes, as soon as you’ve checked they can get out by themselves, then it’s great for them to have free access. I’m sure it helps with their well-being.”

After a couple of minutes, the pups hauled themselves out of the pond and lolloped into the kennel. They pulled themselves on to the trampoline and flopped down on their sides, cuddled up next to each other.

“Well,” said Elspeth, “I think we can safely say they’ve bonded. I should get going, but call me any time if you need anything.”

As soon as she was out of sight, Tom murmured, “How come she’s suddenly being nice to us?”

"I know, it's so weird," said Jasmine. "Maybe she's just a really strange person."

A few minutes later, Dad came through the gate. He stared into the kennel, his eyes wide. "Have you cloned Pearl?"

Jasmine laughed. "Elspeth brought her a friend. He's called Silver."

"So you're setting up a seal sanctuary now? What does Mum think?"

"She thinks it's good for Pearl to have a companion," said Jasmine. Which was true, if not quite the whole truth. "But we're not taking any more. Just these two."

"So you've sealed the deal."

"Dad! You said no more seal jokes."

"Sorry, couldn't resist. That's the last one, I promise."

At four o'clock it was time for Silver's first feed. Jasmine and Tom took two bottles of warm fishy milk out to the pen. They peeped through

the door and saw Pearl and Silver cuddled up together on the trampoline. Flipper lay abandoned on the floor.

"They're so cute together," whispered Jasmine. "But poor Flipper."

"You can't have him back in your room," said Tom. "He absolutely stinks."

"I'll put him in the washing machine. He'll be fine."

As Jasmine opened the door, the pups raised their heads and mewed eagerly. They flopped off the trampoline and shimmied towards the children.

Pearl immediately latched on to Tom's bottle and sucked the milk enthusiastically. Jasmine offered her bottle to Silver. "Here you are, baby. Lovely warm milk."

Silver sniffed the teat and turned away. Jasmine dribbled a little milk on to his lips. He kept his mouth closed.

"Come on, Silver. It's really nice."

But the pup refused to drink. When Pearl had finished her bottle, Tom had a try, but Silver wouldn't open his mouth. They persevered for a long time, but he showed no interest.

"I think he's going to have to be tube-fed," Tom said at last.

Jasmine felt sick. She'd been so sure Silver would take a bottle. What would Mum say when she realised she was going to have to tube-feed him five times a day?

She took a deep breath and went indoors. Nadia was in her study, going through her emails. She swivelled round in her chair as Jasmine entered.

"I was thinking," said Jasmine. "About what you said about sorry not being enough. So I'm going to clear the table every day after tea, and load the dishwasher, and wash up all the pans and stuff. Every day of the holidays."

Nadia looked at the bottle in Jasmine's hand and raised her eyebrows. "So, Silver needs tube feeding, does he?"

How did she know?

"We've tried for ages with the bottle, but he won't even open his mouth. I'm so sorry."

"Well, I'm not surprised. You can keep trying, but Elspeth did say most pups have to be tube-fed. Dad said he'll help, and if you and Tom prepare the milk and wash everything up thoroughly afterwards, the actual feeding shouldn't take long."

"Thank you, Mum," said Jasmine. "Thank you so much."

As they walked downstairs together, she remembered the other thing she had to ask. It probably wouldn't be a good idea to spring any more surprises on Mum.

"By the way," she said, "Elspeth said people need to be educated about how to act around wild seals. And Tom said maybe we could tell the local TV station about Silver and Pearl, and maybe they'd want to come and film them, and then we can tell people how important it is to leave seals alone."

"Right," said Nadia. "So we might be having TV cameras here?"

"Maybe. But we haven't said anything to Elspeth yet. We thought it might be better if you did that."

"Yes," said Nadia. "I think it might."

"But don't tell Manu, whatever you do. And can you make sure he's not here when the TV

people come?"

"TV people?" said Manu, running into the hall. "TV people coming here? Yay, I'm going to be on TV!"

Chapter Eleven
Ready for the Camera

Pearl and Silver grew and thrived. Every day, they put on weight and spent longer in the water. Jasmine and Tom loved watching them play together.

One morning, a week after Silver's arrival, Mum came out to the seal pen, holding her phone.

"Elspeth just called," she said. "The seal sanctuary thought a TV appearance would be very helpful for educating people about seals. They contacted TV South and they want to

come and film the pups."

Jasmine squealed with excitement. "We're going to be on TV! Oh, my goodness, Tom, we're going to be famous!"

On the morning of the visit Jasmine woke very early. The TV crew might want to film her other animals as well as the seals, so they all needed to be groomed and ready for the camera.

By breakfast time she had taken Sky for his walk, mucked out the orchard shelter, fed Dotty, Mistletoe and Truffle and thoroughly groomed them. Tom arrived after breakfast, and they scrubbed out the seals' enclosure. They had already cleaned out the pond and filled it with fresh water the day before.

As they emerged from the pen, the orchard gate rattled open, and they turned to see Manu and Ben, each carrying a stack of cake tins and plastic containers. Manu had a picnic rug tucked under one arm.

"What are you doing?" asked Jasmine.

"It's our museum," said Manu, as he spread the rug on the ground. "For the TV people."

He opened a tin with a flourish, revealing an assortment of animal bones.

"Oh, your bone museum," said Tom.

"Also teeth," said Ben, opening another tin. "And two whole skulls."

"It's a museum and a shop," said Manu. "They can look at the collection and film us talking about it, and they can buy stuff too."

"And we've got a café," said Ben, opening another tin to reveal some misshapen chocolate chip cookies. "Fifty pence each, or three for a pound. You can buy one if there's any left."

"Roman remains are five pounds each," said Manu, pulling the lid off a tin filled with pieces of broken pottery. "Skulls are ten pounds, and bones are two pounds each, or three for five pounds."

"You need to clear this away," said Jasmine. "They're coming to see the seals. They won't want to be distracted by weird stuff you've found in fields."

"And they'll need all this space for their equipment," said Tom. "They'll have massive cameras and microphones."

Mistletoe came over to sniff at the containers, and Ben clamped the lid on the biscuit tin.

"It won't take them long to film the seals," said Manu. "I bet they'll want to film other stuff too."

"Just move it," said Jasmine. "Now."

"Fine, we'll pull the rug back. If the donkey gets off it."

Jasmine coaxed Mistletoe away, and the boys carefully pulled the rug with all its contents to the other side of the orchard.

Suddenly they heard a flurry of barking and shouting. Jasmine spun round.

She froze in terror.

A dog was scrambling over the wire fence round the pond enclosure.

"No!" Jasmine yelled, racing up the orchard.

The dog leaped into the enclosure and pounced on top of Pearl.

"Get off!" Jasmine screamed. "Get off her!"

But the dog opened its mouth and sank its teeth into Pearl's back. The pup cried out, twisting her body and flippers in distress. Silver cowered in the kennel. On the other side of the fence a panicked woman, her arms flailing, desperately called the dog. It took no notice of her.

Jasmine rushed into the pen, dived into the kennel and out of the back door, slamming it behind her to keep Silver safe. The dog snarled and sank its teeth into Pearl's neck. Jasmine grasped its collar and tried to yank it away.

"Get off her! Get off!"

But the dog's jaws stayed clamped to the pup's neck.

"Drop it!" screamed Jasmine, pulling with all her strength on the collar. "Drop it now!"

But the dog didn't budge.

Suddenly a jet of water hit Jasmine in the face. She let go of the collar in shock. Tom had turned on the hose and aimed it at the dog. As Jasmine grabbed the collar again, the water hit the dog's face. It yelped, let go of the seal, slipped out of Jasmine's grasp and bit her hand.

Seizing her chance, Jasmine clutched Pearl and scooped her up, trying to hold her out of reach of the dog. It leaped up and bit Jasmine on the thigh.

"Stop it!" yelled Tom, spraying the hose all over the dog. But the dog was in a frenzy and the water was making it worse.

Clutching the seal pup, Jasmine stood helplessly by the pond. She was trapped. She couldn't open the kennel door in case the dog rushed in and attacked Silver. And there was no other way out.

"I'm coming in!" Tom shouted. He dropped the hose and raced to the pen. Within a few seconds, the kennel door opened and there he was, Silver struggling in his arms.

"Hurry!" he shouted, and Jasmine ran into the kennel and out the other side. Tom slammed the door of the pen behind them, trapping the dog inside.

Numb with shock, they laid the heavy seal pups on the grass and straddled them to keep them safe and still. It took a few seconds to register the presence of Mum, Dad, Elspeth, Manu and Ben, all staring at the scene in horror.

"Oh, Jasmine, you've been bitten!" exclaimed Nadia.

"No, Pearl's been bitten, look. She needs

treating quickly."

"Was it the seal or the dog that bit you?" Nadia asked.

"The dog," said Tom.

For the first time Jasmine looked at her hand and noticed the row of puncture wounds. "Of course it was the dog!" she said indignantly. "Pearl would never bite me."

"It bit your leg, too," said Tom.

"It doesn't hurt. You need to treat Pearl, Mum."

"We need to treat you both," said Nadia. "I'll take Pearl to the surgery for X-rays, but first we must wash your bites. Come on."

"I'll clean Pearl's wounds and get her into a crate," said Elspeth. "I'll check Silver, too. Tom, can you be my assistant?"

"What about the TV people?" asked Manu.

"We'll have to cancel that," said Mum.

Dad strode towards the dog's owner, still standing in shock outside the pen. His face was

tight with anger.

"How did your dog get into the pen?" he asked.

"He climbed the fence. We were just walking past, and he must have seen the seals moving about."

"Why wasn't it on a lead?"

"I didn't think he needed to be. He's very well behaved. He's never done anything like this before."

"That's what all dog owners say when their dog attacks livestock. But it's your responsibility to prevent an attack, and the only way to do that is to keep it on a lead."

"How was I to know there'd be seals here? What are they even doing on a farm?"

"That's not the point. There are free-range chickens here, too. There are ducks. You presumably guessed there'd be animals on a farm? I need your details, please. I'll be informing the council and the police."

Mum ushered Jasmine indoors, so she couldn't

hear any more. Honestly, why were some dog owners so stupid?

"Will Pearl be OK?" she asked.

"I'm sure she will. Let's look at these bites."

Nadia made Jasmine stand in the bath while she examined her and cleaned the bites with warm water from the shower.

"Look!" said Jasmine, pointing out of the window. "The TV people are here."

A large van with "TV SOUTH" in big letters on the side was trundling along the farm track.

Nadia patted the wounds dry. "Dad and Elspeth will sort it out. Now, I'll put a dressing on, and we'll get you some antibiotics. Just to make sure the bites don't get infected."

As soon as Mum had finished, she and Jasmine went out to see the seals. Elspeth had draped a towel over Pearl and was putting her into a crate. Tom was in the kennel with Silver. There was no sign of the dog and his owner or the TV van.

"Are the pups OK?" asked Jasmine.

"Silver's fine," said Elspeth. "But Pearl's got multiple puncture wounds on her neck and round her rear flipper. They should heal as long as they don't get infected, and we can give her antibiotics to prevent infection. But we'll need to do X-rays to find out whether there are any broken bones."

"And if there are?"

"We'll cross that bridge when we come to it," said Mum.

But Jasmine had heard that breezy tone of Nadia's before, and she wasn't going to be fobbed off by it. "Tell me," she said, fixing her eyes on her mother's. "I need to know the worst that could happen."

Nadia glanced at Elspeth. "You've got a lot

more experience with seals than I have. What do you think?"

Elspeth took a deep breath. "Well, we can treat the bites, but if her flipper's damaged, that's much trickier. We might be able to pin a fracture, but damage to the joints or ligaments or nerves is harder to mend."

"And if you can't mend it?" Jasmine asked.

Elspeth took a deep breath. "We have a policy of not keeping seals in captivity. So if the flipper was damaged badly enough that Pearl couldn't live in the wild, then I'm afraid we'd have to put her to sleep."

Jasmine stared at her. "But that won't happen, will it? She'll be fine, won't she?"

"I'm sure she will," said Mum. "Elspeth, can you come too? Let's get her to the surgery."

Chapter Twelve
News

The waiting was terrible. Dad made sandwiches for lunch, but no one had much of an appetite. Manu and Ben's museum lay abandoned in the orchard. The boys were so shocked about the seal attack that they hadn't even eaten the cookies. Tom and Jasmine couldn't eat at all. Every time Jasmine thought about Pearl and what would happen to her if her flipper was damaged, she felt sick.

As she was loading the dishwasher, the phone rang. She raced across the kitchen and snatched

up the receiver.

"Hello?"

"Hi, Jasmine," said Nadia. "It's good news. We've X-rayed Pearl and she has no broken bones or serious damage."

Jasmine sank down on the floor in relief. "Oh, thank goodness! So she'll be all right?"

"She should be, yes. We've given her antibiotics and pain relief, so she just needs to recover in peace for a while. Elspeth's fetching a quarantine crate from the seal hospital to put in the kennel. Can you ask Dad to fix up a heat lamp, please? I'm going to bring her back now."

"Oh, that's so good. We'll get everything ready."

Jasmine put the phone down, and she and Tom jumped and whooped for joy. Then Tom went to tell Manu and Ben the wonderful news, while Jasmine hurried off to find Michael.

"When my dad built this kennel," he said, hammering a metal hook into a roof beam, "he'd never have dreamed that one day there'd be two seal pups living here. Can you get me an extension lead, Jasmine? There should be one in the garage."

Jasmine plugged the lead into a socket in the scullery and ran the cable out to the kennel. Dad hung the heat lamp from the hook. Silver took a great interest in all the activity and sucked Dad's boot while he worked.

"Honestly, Silver, I don't understand you," said Jasmine. "Why do you love sucking on wellies but refuse to suck a bottle full of milk?"

"It's nearly feeding time," said Tom, who had appeared at the door of the pen. "Let's try him with the bottle again."

As Tom went into the house to heat the milk, Elspeth's van drew up in the yard. Jasmine helped her carry a large high-sided plastic crate into the kennel. It had an open top, and they placed it directly under the heat lamp. It was a bit of a squash with the trampoline as well.

"Pearl can rest quietly in there while her wounds heal," said Elspeth. "Keep it very clean and keep her wounds very clean as well. Check on them regularly to see how they're healing and send me photos if you're worried about anything."

At the sound of Nadia's car pulling up in the yard, Jasmine hurried out and opened the boot. Pearl's huge dark eyes gazed out at her, and she greeted Jasmine with a little call.

"Oh, Pearl," said Jasmine. "We're so, so glad to have you safely home."

Tom brought out the milk and Jasmine fed Pearl over the side of the crate. To her great relief the pup guzzled as eagerly as ever.

"That must be a good sign," she said.

"She's so brave," said Tom. "To recover so quickly after that awful attack."

"She's amazing," said Jasmine, looking fondly at the pup. "I bet when you go out to sea, Pearl, you'll be the bravest hunter of all."

"How will they know how to hunt for fish when they're released?" Tom asked Elspeth. "If they've never done it before?"

"We don't really know how they know," Elspeth said, "but it's probably a combination of instinct and copying other seals. That's why we release pups close to a seal colony, so they can join it and learn from older seals. And we tag all our pups before releasing them, so we can track

their progress. They've all been seen foraging for fish, and most of them have been seen swimming or hauling out with other seals. So they clearly work out what to do."

Silver still refused to take a bottle, despite his eagerness to suck on Tom's trousers. After Dad had tube-fed him, he fetched a roll of netting and made a roof for the pond enclosure.

"I should have roofed it in the first place," he said. "But I never thought a dog would scale a six-foot fence to attack the pups."

Jasmine turned to Elspeth. "I guess Pearl shouldn't swim for a while, should she?"

"Well, actually," said Elspeth, "saltwater is very good for healing wounds. With a wounded animal that's otherwise healthy, we've found it's good to have them in saltwater as much as possible. So we can add salt to their pool, and then you can let them swim together."

"That's good," said Tom. "They'll be sad enough to be separated when they're sleeping, so at least they can be together in the pool."

When they went to check on the pups later, there was no sign of Silver in the pen or on the trampoline. They peered into the crate and Jasmine's face broke into a smile.

"Oh," whispered Tom. "That's so cute."

The pups were snuggled up together, side by side under the heat lamp, fast asleep. The children tiptoed out so as not to disturb them.

"How did Silver get in the crate?" Jasmine wondered. "He must have climbed right up the side and hauled himself over the top."

"Unless he bounced really high on the trampoline and jumped in."

Jasmine laughed. "I wish we could have seen it."

"Do you think it's OK for him to be in there? What if he accidentally infects Pearl's wounds?"

"Let's phone Elspeth and ask."

Elspeth said that as long as they checked Pearl's wounds regularly for signs of infection, and made sure the seals and their pen were kept spotlessly clean, then it should be fine if Silver joined Pearl in the crate.

"Just move the heat lamp out of reach," she said. "We don't want Silver burning himself when he gets in and out. But I'm sure it will help Pearl to have him with her. They clearly love each other's company."

Chapter Thirteen
Entirely at Home

The pups grew so fast, with the increasing amounts of milk they were given, that they were soon too heavy for Jasmine and Tom to lift, and Dad and Mum had to put them on the scales each morning.

Pearl's wounds healed well and she was able to leave the quarantine crate. Elspeth phoned regularly to check on their progress. And in the last week of August, when Jasmine told her that both pups weighed over twenty kilograms, Elspeth said, "I think they're ready to be released."

Jasmine had always known this day would come, and of course she wanted the pups to be free, but it felt unbearably sad knowing that Pearl and Silver would swim away and she would never see them again.

"I've got an idea," said Tom. "How about we phone the TV station and ask if they want to film the release? They were keen last time, and they were really shocked about the dog attack. I bet they'd come."

Tom was right. TV South did want to tell the story of Pearl and Silver and film their release. They arranged to meet at the beach car park on the final day of the holidays.

On the morning of the release Jasmine gave Pearl her very last bottle of sardine milkshake.

"I can't believe we'll never feed them again," said Tom, stroking Silver's head.

A lump formed in Jasmine's throat as she set down the empty bottle and stroked Pearl's sleek back. She screwed up her face to stop herself

from crying, but a tear fell on to the little seal's fur.

"That must be Elspeth," said Tom at the sound of a vehicle driving into the yard. Jasmine brushed the tears away with her sleeve.

Elspeth introduced Jason, another Marine Mammal Medic who had come to help with the release. The children watched as they fixed satellite tags to the pups.

"That's so cool," said Manu. "What do they do?"

"They use GPS and mobile phone technology to tell us where the seals travel to, how deep they dive and where they haul out," said Elspeth. "It really helps with seal conservation, because we can tell where they're finding food and what their main habitats are, and then we can try to make sure those places are protected."

Elspeth and Jason expertly manoeuvred the seals into crates, and they set off in convoy to the beach, Mum's car following Elspeth's van.

"There's the TV van!" said Manu excitedly, as they drove into the car park. Jasmine's stomach fluttered at the thought of talking to the TV interviewer.

The presenter, camerawoman and sound man were already setting up on the beach when Elspeth, Jason, Nadia and Michael set down the crates facing the sea. The TV people introduced themselves and cooed over the pups for a few minutes, and then the presenter, who was called Candice, said she'd like to ask Elspeth, Jasmine and Tom a few questions. She asked Jasmine's parents if they'd like to be interviewed, too, but Michael shook his head and Nadia said, "No, we'll leave it to the experts."

"What about me?" asked Manu.

"You didn't do anything," said Jasmine, but the presenter smiled and said, "Of course I'll interview you."

Manu beamed, and Jasmine and Tom gave each other a look that said, "She'll regret that decision." Jasmine noticed a skull stuffed into one of Manu's bulging jacket pockets, and a bone sticking out of the other.

"We'll let you focus on the release first, and ask you questions afterwards," said Candice.

"Everybody needs to stand well back," said Elspeth, taking charge. "From this point on they're wild animals again. Jasmine and Tom, would you like to open the crates?"

Jasmine and Tom nodded and stepped forward. With the camera trained on them from a distance they kneeled beside the crates and said their goodbyes.

"Have a great time and catch lots of fish," said Tom. "And stay away from people and dogs."

Jasmine gazed at the pups' beautiful gentle faces peering out of their crates.

"I'm going to miss you both so much. It's been amazing looking after you. You've been the bravest, sweetest, loveliest seal pups ever. Have a wonderful life out in the sea."

Tom looked at her. "Now?"

"Now," said Jasmine.

They opened the crates.

Elspeth had told them that some pups made straight for the sea, while others were more cautious and reluctant. Jasmine had worried that Silver and Pearl, so used to human company, wouldn't want to leave their safe,

familiar world for the wild and unknown water. After all, Pearl had never even seen the sea!

The pups shuffled out of their crates. On the pebbly beach they stopped and turned to each other. They sniffed the air. Then, as if in unspoken agreement, they shimmied together across the stones towards the sea and plunged straight into the lapping waves. They frolicked at the shallow water's edge, flipping on to their backs and weaving over and under each

other. Then they swam further out, their heads bobbing above the waves and disappearing again. They looked entirely at home out there in the endless shimmering fish-filled water that stretched away to the bright horizon.

Chapter Fourteen
All Grown Up

When they got home, Jasmine walked straight past the empty kennel, her eyes to the ground. At some point she would have to clean it out and remove the tarpaulin and the trampoline, but she couldn't bear to think about that yet. Instead, she and Tom took Sky for a long walk by the river.

"Wow," said Jasmine. "Look how big the cygnets are!"

The family of swans was sailing elegantly down the river. The cygnets had grey-brown

feathers instead of fluffy down, and their wings were fast developing.

"Soon you'll be all grown-up," said Jasmine, "and you'll fly off and have new lives of your own."

Tom looked at his watch. "We'd better head back. The news will be on soon."

Jasmine's stomach flipped. She was going to see herself on television!

Mum had let Manu make pizzas for tea, and the kitchen was an unbelievable mess. They all carried their plates into the living room to eat in front of the TV. The dough was very thick and not really cooked in the middle, but apart from that the pizzas weren't bad. But the news seemed to go on forever. They finished their pizzas and there was still no mention of the seals.

"What if they've decided not to show them?" said Jasmine.

"I bet they'll put them last," said Tom. "They always do a nice thing at the end."

"And finally," said the presenter, smiling at the camera, "two rescued seal pups were released back into the sea at Easthaven today..."

Jasmine gave a squeal of excitement. Everyone leaned forward eagerly, and Manu bounced up and down on the sofa.

The screen showed Jasmine and Tom crouching on the beach beside the seal crates, and then cut to Candice.

"Two Sussex schoolchildren have spent their summer holidays caring for a pair of orphaned seal pups," Candice said. "So it was a bittersweet moment when the pups finally made their way back to sea today."

The picture changed to Silver and Pearl lolloping into the sea, and then cut to Jasmine and Tom standing awkwardly on the beach.

"Jasmine, your mum's a vet and you live on a farm, so you were able to offer a home to the seal pups," said Candice. "Tell us what happened and how you looked after them."

Jasmine squirmed as she watched the interview. It was so weird to see and hear herself on TV.

Candice asked Tom a question next, and then the camera cut to Elspeth. When they were at the beach, Jasmine and Tom had been so occupied with watching the seals that they hadn't seen Elspeth being interviewed, so now they listened with interest.

"As a Marine Mammal Medic, you rescue a lot of seal pups," Candice said. "Is human interference a growing problem, and what should the public do about it?"

"Unfortunately," said Elspeth, "we're seeing more and more cases of seals being abandoned because of human disturbance. These two pups were typical victims. Not only were their mothers frightened into leaving them because of people getting too close, but during their

rehabilitation they were also attacked by an unleashed dog. We have so many cases like this at the moment that our seal hospital currently has no space to take in more casualties."

"So it was lucky that you found a family with the space and expertise to help," said Candice.

"Very lucky. It needs a trained Marine Mammal Medic or vet to rescue and rehabilitate a seal. But the credit for Pearl's survival is actually due to the children, Jasmine and Tom."

Jasmine and Tom stared at each other in amazement. Elspeth was giving them the credit?

"If it wasn't for them," said Elspeth, "alerting us in the first place and then risking their own safety to rescue her from a savage attack, she would never have survived, and we wouldn't be seeing this wonderful sight today."

The camera panned round to show Silver and Pearl gambolling in the sea.

"Thanks to the efforts of the rescuers, these two young seals have a life of freedom ahead

of them," said Candice. "This is Candice Okoro reporting from Easthaven."

The picture cut back to the studio presenter.

"Hey!" exclaimed Manu. "They didn't show my interview!"

"Of course they didn't," said Jasmine. "You just talked about your bone collection and tried to sell the presenter a fox skull."

"You have to admit it was enterprising," said Dad. "One day, when Manu's a millionaire, we'll all be sorry we didn't take him more seriously."

After tea, Jasmine and Tom took Sky out to the orchard. Mum was already there, picking the ripe plums.

"Look!" said Tom, pointing to the pool.

Dad had taken the fence down, and Button was sailing happily on the little pond, while Mistletoe and Dotty drank the water. Truffle lay stretched out on her side in the evening sunlight.

Jasmine's face broke into a smile. "You four won't ever leave me, will you? And nor will you, Sky."

"I wonder where Pearl and Silver are now," said Tom.

"I guess you'll be able to find out from Elspeth, since they're tagged," said Mum. "You can get regular updates. It's almost like they can phone home."

"Our little babies, out in the big wide world," said Jasmine. "I hope they'll be OK."

"Most little babies leave the nest eventually," said Mum. "You just have to do your best for them while they're with you. And you certainly did that with Pearl and Silver. I think you can be very proud parents."